The Rhino Who Swallowed a Storm

by **LeVar Burton**

& Susan Schaefer Bernardo

Illustrations by Courtenay Fletcher

READING RAINBOW.

BURBANK, CALIFORNIA

First Edition: September 2014
10 9 8 7 6 5 4 3 2
ISBN 978-0-9905395-0-6 (hardcover)

Visit us at www.ReadingRainbow.com

Book and jacket design by Courtenay Fletcher
Printed and bound in the USA

For the Rhino in us all.

~ L. B.

For the storytellers
who inspire imagination and courage
and for my Sweet Girl, always.

~ C. F.

Whatever the weather,
we can face it together . . . with love!

~ S. B.

A special thank you to our
talented editor, Sangita Patel.

In the middle of the morning, Mica Mouse trembled under her blanket. A storm boomed outside her window. Rain crashed against the glass. Wind rattled the shutters.

More than anything else, Mica was afraid of storms. A year before, a powerful hurricane had destroyed her home.

"I'm scared, Papa," she said.

"We are safe, Mica. This storm will pass soon," said Papa. "Would you like me to read you a story? I know just the one to help you feel better."

Mica loved books—and Papa's gentle voice soothed in a way that made her forget all about the thunder.

Papa opened the book and began.

Long, long ago . . .

before there were words,
animals roamed in bountiful herds.
Little Rhinoceros lived happy and free,
exploring mountains and meadows, rivers and trees.

His world was delightful
and chock full of magic—
until out of the blue,
the magic turned tragic.

A storm swept through the valley,
turning bright sky to black.
A flash flood came raging,
no time to react.

    Lost in the thundering,
        no time for wondering,
    chaos and lightning,
        fury so frightening,
    earth quaking,
        him shaking,
    water rumbling,
        him tumbling,
    raggedy jaggedy,
        senseless calamity . . .

The storm crashed through his world
and tore it apart,
and took away **everything**
dear to his heart.

Rhino was stunned by the terrible scene,
death and destruction all through the ravine.
Enraged by the pain of such a great loss,
Rhino acted without a thought to the cost.

Rhino looked at his world, all tattered and torn,
stood out on the ledge and . . . swallowed the storm.

Inside his belly, he felt the storm growing.
Inside his head, he heard howling and blowing.
Like a tornado he spun as the storm raged inside,
growing bigger and bigger and wider than wide.

When he finally stopped, when he regained control,
he was at the very bottom of a very deep hole.

"What to do?" Rhino worried as rain dripped down his face.
"I'm lost and I'm lonely and in such a dark place."
At just the right moment to comfort and guide him,
a spider dropped down and dangled beside him.

"The world up above is shattered and gray,
but it's where you belong, so you must find a way
to let that storm out and move through your sorrow.
You'll find many helpers on your road to tomorrow."

Oh, but that hole
        was dreadfully deep. . .
And the walls all around him
        were slippery steep.
Rhino tried to climb out
        but was losing all hope,
when Kangaroo heard him
        and threw down a rope.
Though Rhino was heavy
        from the weight of the storm,
they towed him right up,
        got him safe, dry, and warm.

"We're **strong** and **steady** and always ready.

When danger strikes, we **hop** to it!

Fire or flood, snow or mud—

when **help** is needed, we'll pull **you** through it."

Watching those heroes do what they did best
gave Rhino the strength to set off on his quest.

That storm he was clutching made him buzzy and blurry.
It kept his brain foggy and filled him with worry.

"Where do I go? What do I do?
How will I ever make it through?"

"After every dark night, there comezzz a new day.

Beeee kind, do your best, and you'll find your way.

Up comezzz the sun. There are steps to complete.

There izzzn't a map. Just follow your feet."

Rhino followed his feet to a wallowing spot,
where he plopped on a rock and had a deep thought.

"I'm tired of caging the wind and the rain,
exhausted from holding this anger and pain."

"We're all on this earth to learn and to grow,"
a wise old tortoise chimed in from below.

"Allowing yourself to start feeling your feelings

is the very first step on the journey toward healing."

"It doesn't much matter if you're fast or you're slow, if you want to move forward, just trust and let go."

Rhino shook and shimmied and stomped in the muck,
and just as he hoped, that storm came unstuck!
At first one little raindrop leaked out of his eye,
then Rhino let go and had a good cry.

His tears formed a river that flowed to the sea,
where a pod of whales swam happy and free.
"I do feel better," Rhino thought as he drifted.
Then up swam a whale, and Rhino was lifted.

"If you ever feel blue," the whale said with a spout, "remember to **breathe**. Breathe in and breathe out.

Sing your own song and take it deep, deep, deep . . . then rise above with a joyful **leap!**"

As he floated home on a gentle wave,
Rhino felt calm and strong and brave.
His vision was clear like the sky above,
and he looked at his world through eyes
filled with love.

He thanked the kind spider and the brave kangaroo,
and all of the others who'd helped him through.
He was glad to know that if he ever lost hope,
they'd lend him a hand or throw him a rope.

He had journeyed his journey
a very long way,
to find the light
in a world turned gray.
He'd swallowed a storm
with no thought to the cost.
He'd felt all alone.
He'd been tumbled and tossed.

Life would bring changes, beginnings and ends,
but he had faith in himself—and faith in his friends.
As they curled up together, he felt loved and protected,
and he dreamed of a world that was safe and connected.

He understood now it was love that mattered.
Love could never be lost. Love could never be shattered.

Papa closed the book and gave Mica a hug.

"I know it was scary when our home was destroyed last winter," said Papa. "Bad things happen sometimes, and we can't always control that."

"But we had lots of helpers," said Mica. "Just like Rhino did."

"That's right, Little One," Papa said in his gentle way. "You're never really alone when bad things happen. There are family and friends, even people we don't know, who are always there to help us through tough times."

GOUDA TIMES

Take a deeper look inside this book . . .

1. At the beginning of the book, Mica Mouse is scared by a thunderstorm. Can you think of a time when you have been frightened?

2. In the story, swallowing a storm is a metaphor for holding in your feelings. Have you ever had emotions swirling inside of you like a tornado? What are some ways you let them out?

3. Did you notice that after Rhino swallows the storm, the illustrations turn gray to show Rhino's sadness? How does Rhino learn to see the color in the world again?

4. After Rhino falls into a very deep hole, he feels lost and lonely and stuck. Have you ever felt like Rhino? What did you do? What gave you hope?

5. The whale tells Rhino to "sing your own song." What are some ways you express *your* feelings?

6. Once Rhino lets out the storm, he is able to see his world "through eyes filled with love." What are things you love about your world?

7. Rhino meets many helpers on his journey. Who helps and encourages you? How do you help others?

8. Mica feels better after reading a book with her papa. What books or activities comfort you and make you feel better?